I CAN SHARE

Sarah Read

Go here to get

https://bookhip.com/HQWTBQ

"The Anxious Monster" for FREE!

THIS BOOK BELONGS TO

....

....

Matthew woke up feeling good and looking forward to the day.
He got dressed and bounded down the stairs; he was eager to play.
Should he play with his cars first or go out into the yard?
With so many ideas, making a decision was hard.

As Matthew walked past the den, he noticed Mia inside.
She was happily playing with something and beaming with pride.
She adored her little toy doggy; it was a robot too.
It was so clever, it did whatever Mia told it to do.

Matthew was fascinated by Mia's tempting new toy.
He suddenly became a curious and jealous little boy.
He went over and grabbed the toy then ran out to the yard.
This upset Mia so much that she started crying very hard.

Dad heard the commotion and went out into the yard to see
Matthew with the doggy and Mia as sad as can be.
Dad took the toy and gave it back to Mia, then asked Matthew,
"How do you think you'd feel if your sister did the same to you?"

Matthew thought about it for a while then said, "I think I would feel mad. I just wanted to play with the toy. I didn't want her to feel bad."
Dad said, "If you want to play with Mia's toys, you'll have to ask to share. You must not take something without asking. That isn't being fair."

"Ask Mia if you can have a turn when she's finished with her toy.
Act like a responsible brother, a thoughtful and polite big boy."
Matthew realized he shouldn't have behaved the way he had.
He apologized to Mia, then made a promise to her and Dad.

Matthew agreed to not grab Mia's toys. Instead, he'd ask to play.
He would wait until she finished, even if it took all day.
Dad left them both out in the yard and Matthew did as he'd said.
He let Mia finish playing and played with his own toys instead.

Matthew built his cars a racing track that spread out very far.
Mia looked on with interest as he raced his favorite car.
Matthew was counting how long it took for each car to get to the end.
Mia wanted to get involved and so did her new little friend.

"This is my robotic puppy," Mia said as she approached the track.
"He does tricks and likes to have his tummy tickled while lying on his back.
We could take turns looking after him and playing with the cars too."
Mia passed her toy to Matthew who then placed his cars in a queue.

They played together for the rest of the morning, having so much fun.
Matthew had forgotten how horribly his morning had begun.
From now on, whenever Matthew wants his little sister to share,
He asks for permission and waits patiently. He always does what's fair.

Thank you

What Did You Think of *I Can Share*?

Thank you for purchasing this book. I know you could have picked any number of books to read, but you picked this book and for that I am extremely grateful.

If you like the book... and if you'd be willing to spare just two or three minutes... would you be willing to share your review of the book on Amazon?

If you would, it would mean the absolute world to me!

Thank you SO much. This helps to get the book into as many hands as possible, helping other parents and educators!

I really appreciate all your support!

Sarah Read
children's book author

Go here to get

https://BookHip.com/HQWTBQ

"The Anxious Monster" for FREE!

18516584R00021